Mail Order
The Bride's !
Chance Christmas

By
Faith Johnson

Clean and Wholesome Western Historical Romance

Table of Contents

Unsolicited Testimonials

By **Glaidene Ramsey**
★★★★★ I so enjoy reading Faith Johnson's stories. This Bride and groom met as she arrived in town. They were married and then the story begins.!!!! Enjoy

By **Voracious Reader**
★★★★★ "Great story of love and of faith. The hardships we may have to go through and how with faith, and God's help we can get through them" -

By **Glaidene's reads**
★★★★★ "Faith Johnson is a five star writer. I have read a majority of her books. I enjoyed the story and hope you will too!!!!!"

By **Kirk Statler**
★★★★★ I liked the book. A different twist because she wasn't in contract with anyone when she went. She went. God provided for her needs. God blessed her above and beyond.

By **Amazon Customer**
★★★★★ Great clean and easy reading, a lot of fun for you to know ignores words this is crazy so I'll not reviewing again. Let me tell it and go

By **Kindle Customer**
★★★★★ Wonderful story. You have such a way of showing people that opposite do attack. Both in words and action. I am glad that I found your books.

Just to say thanks for checking our works we like to gift you

Our Exclusive Never Before Released Books

100% FREE!

Please GO TO

`http://cleanromancepublishing.com/gift`

And get your FREE gift

Thanks for being such a wonderful client.

Chapter One

"Good morning, Eleanor," Adam, the shopkeeper, chirped as the young woman entered the general store, his eyes bright. "It's good to see you! I feel as though you haven't graced me with your presence in quite a while." Though his smile remained, the shopkeeper's eyes softened. "How is your father? I heard about the assaults he recently endured. Is he well?"

Eleanor Monfrey offered the man a friendly smile and gave a slight nod, her basket perched delicately on her arm. "Yes, my father is well," she told him sweetly. "I am greatly appreciative of your concern." She allowed her eyes to drop, taking on an aura of sadness. "It was terrible what happened to him, really."

The shopkeeper nodded along with her. "It really was." He hesitated, his eyes gauging her. "Perhaps… perhaps it might behoove your father to stay away from the gambling halls. Those establishments only attract individuals of bad character."

Against her will, Eleanor's eye twitched. "Perhaps," she agreed.

"Well, it isn't my place to say." The friendly smile returned to Adam's face, and he gestured to the store. "Is there anything I can help you with? Do you have a list of the things I can grab for you?"

"No, no," she said quickly as another patron entered the store and greeted Adam.

"I'm fine on my own, thank you. I remember my way around."

"As you wish. Please do not let me interrupt you. Make sure you grab a half pound of raisins; it'll be on me. My wife dried them out herself."

"I will do that, thank you," she told him gratefully, genuine in her gratitude. Giving him one last nod, she slowly made her way through the store, grabbing the items that she needed.

From all of her encounters with him, Adam seemed like a kind man. He had always treated her with kindness and respect, and his wife, Helen, was just as warm and kind. It filled Eleanor with guilt, knowing what she had to do.

Walking along the pathways and passing by the shelves filled with food and dry supplies, there were plenty of moments when Eleanor was out of Adam's view. Not that he was watching her intently or suspicious of her; her wide blue eyes, shorter stature, and small, warm smile gave her the look of innocence. No one would suspect her of anything.

Under a simple, thin petticoat, Eleanor had several tie-on pockets around her waist. As she weighed half a pound of raisins into a small sack and placed it in her basket, she filled one of the tie-on pockets with nearly a pound more of raisins. She was thin enough that most of her clothing hung loose on her frame, so there was plenty of room to hide stolen goods.

There was a trick to it, obviously. For one, she needed to remain out of sight. Fortunately for her, Adam was busy helping out the other patron, so the risk of her getting caught was low. Eleanor also needed to be cautious about what she stole. It couldn't be something expensive that Adam would notice right away. It couldn't be too heavy; otherwise, her range of motion would be minimized. And whatever she stole couldn't make noise. If she stole something in a small tin, it needed to be in a separate pocket, and it couldn't be beside a pocket containing another container.

She stood before a bin of coffee beans, sighing and reaching for another small sack to fill. As much as she wished she could steal coffee beans, they rattled against each other and made too much noise. Trying to steal them would be too much of a risk. So instead, it was one more thing for her to buy, one more thing for her to spend what little money she had on.

Coffee beans were one of the main staples her father demanded to be present in the house at all times, and she wouldn't chance getting a beating.

Her pockets full of raisins, candies, and other goodies, Eleanor made her way back to the main counter, her smile wide and innocent. "It'll just be these today," she told Adam, handing over the coins for the goods.

Giving her the change, a soft smile crept up Adam's lips, and he gently placed a chocolate goodie from his counter in her basket. "This will be on me," he told her, and the guilt ate at her once more.

She murmured a quick thank you and hurried out of the shop and into the cold. Snow was still falling from the sky, albeit lightly, but she knew it could pick up at any time. Pulling her coat more tightly around her, she hurried home to where her father was waiting for her.

She made a stop at the Morrisons', who lived only a block or so down from her. Connor Morrison was a widow, and he often needed clothes washed or mended. She was more than happy to take on any task he may have.

After knocking on his front door, it cracked open, revealing Connor's youngest son, Albert. The boy stood in the doorway, half of his hand in his mouth as he stared up at her. "Hello there," she laughed, crouching down to his level. "I'm looking for your father."

There was the sound of boots clonking against wood, and then a dirty Connor appeared, his expression crabby. "Who—," he began, before realizing it was Eleanor and sighing. "Hello, dear."

"Mr. Morrison," she said with a polite nod as she stood. "I thought I would stop by to check on you, see if you needed anything."

Gifting her with a tired smile, he nodded. "I do, in fact. Yesterday, my pants got caught on a nail and tore a large hole. I also have some other clothing items with general wear and tear. If you want to come by tomorrow morning, I'll have everything gathered for you then. Right now, the boys and I are getting ready for supper.

Eleanor nodded with understanding. She had a stew on the stove that she needed to return to. "Absolutely. Have a good evening, Mr. Morrison."

"You as well, Eleanor." Before she stepped away, she fished the chocolate candy from her basket and handed it to the young boy with a wink.

***

Eleanor had barely taken two steps into her house when her father yanked the basket from her arms, mumbling about how long the trip to the store had taken her as he stomped toward the kitchen. She stood by the door for another few seconds, doing her best to calm her breathing before closing the door and joining him. Her anger would only fuel him.

The bruising on her father's face was beginning to subside; the deep coloring that was once a dark blue and purple was starting to fade into an unsightly yellow. As she watched him, he dug his hand into the sack of raisins and shoveled a handful into his mouth. "What are you doing buying raisins for?" he asked her gruffly. "It's a waste of money!"

"I didn't buy them," she responded quietly, removing all the tie-on pockets from her person and gently setting them on the table. "They were a gift from the shopkeeper."

He ignored her words, ruffling through the tie-on pockets and shaking his head with disappointment. "This is all?" he demanded, gesturing to the table. "You've been gone two hours, and this was all you managed to grab? No cigars, no chewing tobacco, nothing?"

"I can't take those things," she reminded him softly as she moved to check on the pot of stew. It smelled delicious, and she inhaled a deep breath of its scent. "Those things are behind the counter. I told you this."

Quietly cursing, her father shook his head and sat down at the table with force, slapping it with the palm of his hand. "Well, serve me!" he barked. "I've been waiting for too long."

Silently, Eleanor did as he requested, holding her tongue as she always did.

"What about your wages?" he asked as she set a steaming bowl in front of him.

She stiffened and then quickly tried to relax to hide it. She needed to be careful about her response. "They're already gone. I used them for rent."

"Funny that is, seeing that rent isn't due for another two weeks." He stared at her coldly, and she swallowed hard. She couldn't afford to give him that money.

"Father, it's for rent," she pleaded, and he slapped the table again, this time with more force.

"And in two weeks, you will have more wages for rent!" he snapped. "Where is the money?"

As she stared at him, debating whether or not to tell him, she noticed his fists clench.

His knuckles, much like his face, were cut and bruised. If he would happily jump into a fight with the stranger over gambling winnings, he would not bat an eye at striking her.

"It's In the coffee tin," she finally told him, gesturing to the cupboard. Eleanor turned her back on him as he stood, the chair scraping against the wood. Snagging the money, he tossed the tin to the side and muttered something about being back before heading out the front door, his bowl of stew untouched.

He had been like this as long as Eleanor remembered. She sighed and picked up the tin from the floor, wondering if he would ever change.

As far back as her memories went, it had always been her and him. Her mother died early, or so her father claimed; Eleanor wouldn't be surprised if the woman had run off. This left her father to raise Eleanor all on his own.

He was by no means a good man. He was a gambler and a fighter; he rarely held a job, and when he was employed, all of his earnings went towards his gambling. Eleanor remembered always being hungry as a child and rarely having a roof over her head.

He taught her how to steal young, forcing her to do so to help support them. She was a young girl, so he figured no one would ever suspect her, and he was correct. She had never gotten caught.

But just because Eleanor was good at what she did didn't mean she didn't feel bad about having to do it. She was taking from good, honest people who depended on their income. She knew it was wrong what she was doing. She wanted to stop, but her father wouldn't let her.

Eleanor started working young, starting as a maid and an errand girl. She did her best to put the money towards food and rent, but her father always took most of her wages from her. So, she started lying about her wages, hiding what she could. That was a few years ago, and by now, she had managed to put a good amount away.

Initially, she put the money aside to afford food, but now it had a greater purpose. She wanted to leave. She would never get anywhere if she continued to live with her father.

She was determined to escape her past in the city and start a new life on the open prairies. She wasn't going to let anything stop her.

Chapter Two

Eleanor shivered as she clutched the letter in her gloved hand, standing at the edge of the bustling city street. Her breath formed frosty clouds in the chill air, and she pulled her coat tighter around her slender frame. The streets were alive with laughter, but Eleanor's heart was beating quickly with excitement.

In her hands, she held a letter from Henry Winters. He was a widowed farmer in the open prairie, raising a young girl all on his own. He was looking for a wife to help him raise his child, as well as aid him in taking on farm duties. While Eleanor had never lived on a farm, she had worked many jobs on farms over the years and knew her way around fairly well.

The letter was a response to one she had sent him several weeks before, inquiring about the matrimonial ad he had placed in the *Matrimonial News*. Within his letter, he thanked her for her interest and admitted that she had been the first person to respond to his ad, a revelation that saddened Eleanor. It seemed as though not many women were willing to take on the care of a young girl. Eleanor herself had no experience in raising children, but she was quite fond of them and was certain it couldn't be too hard. After all, many women did it regularly.

Really though, Henry had been chosen at random; he was the first matrimonial ad Eleanor had laid her eyes on. Wherever she ended up, she was sure it would be better than where she currently was. She needed to leave soon.

It was time for her to leave her father. Within Henry's letter was an invitation to join him at his homestead, and Eleanor was going to accept. It was not going to be difficult for her to leave home; her father wasn't there half the time, and when he was there, he was often asleep. She'd thought she would feel more guilty about leaving her father, but instead, she was filled with an almost overwhelming sense of relief. No longer would her father be plaguing her life and forcing her to steal from others.

He was strong and a fighter; he would survive just fine without her.

She stuffed the letter deep into one of the tie-on pockets, determined to keep it hidden from her father. She would not give him any hint that she was leaving. There is no doubt in her mind that he would do anything to stop her, considering she provided most of the food and income.

Right after she picked up the letter from the post office, Eleanor immediately wrote Henry back and sent it off, writing to Henry about her intention to join him. It would take a few weeks to get a response from him, but by then, she should be ready to leave. She didn't intend on taking much with her, just whatever money she had stashed away and a sack with some food.

Her fingers growing numb from the cold, Eleanor rubbed her hands together and shoved them deep into her coat pockets, heading home. There was no work for her to do today. She had already checked, so off to home she went to begin dinner and do some cleaning.

As she walked up the path to the house, she noticed several candles lit inside the windows. That meant her father was home. He was likely asleep, so she would have to be quiet while working.

She was not prepared for the sight that greeted her upon stepping inside. There was no wood in the fireplace, the chill within the home making her shiver. The few shelves in the main room, which were stocked with books, supplies, and a few canned food items, were thrown to the floor with their contents scattered.

Fearing that a stranger had invaded their space and robbed them, Eleanor ran through the house, seeing other rooms in a similar state. *My money*, she realized, rushing to her own room. The thought of someone taking her money from her was a terrifying one. All her hard work was at risk.

The door to her bedroom was open, and when she stepped foot inside, she saw her father sitting on her bed, holding a small, familiar tin in his lap. It was the same tin she had hidden under piles of clothing in her dresser, the one that held her savings.

"What are you doing?" she whispered, frozen in the doorway. Had he caused this mess?

He held up the small tin, shaking it. The coins within rattled. "What is this?" he asked her quietly.

"I –" The truth of the situation dawned on her, and Eleanor looked at her father with a mix of shock and revulsion. How could he? "Did you do this?" she demanded, gesturing behind her to the rest of the house, which lay in disarray. "You made that mess? Why have you gone through my things? What cause have I given you to not trust me?"

"Why have you hidden money from me?" he snapped back at her, standing with the tin still clutched in his hands. "What are you planning?"

"Nothing!" she lied through her teeth, clenching her hands by her side. How dare he go through her things?

As angry as she was, Eleanor was also filled with dread. That was all the money she had saved up for a few years; it would take her a long time to save it again. Without that tin, she would have nothing.

"Then why are you hiding it?" he shouted at her, reaching out to grab her roughly and pull her closer. She stood, frozen with fear, as he yelled in her face. His cheeks were a deep red, and his eyes were aflame with a dangerous anger.

"It's just savings," she whispered, doing her best to pull away from him and failing. She worried he was going to lay his hands on her.

"I don't think it is!" he continued, his grip on her tightening as she tried to free herself from his grasp. "I think you're trying to leave, Eleanor. I think you're planning on running away."

"No!"

"Do you take me for a fool?" He shook her so hard her teeth felt like they were rattling in her head. "I know that you despise me and the life we have! You want to leave me, I know it!"

He was correct, of course. But before Eleanor could say anything, he continued. "You're not going anywhere," he told her, lowering his voice into a growl. "If you even think of leaving, I'll turn you into the sheriff. They've caught onto the petty theft you've been committing, though they haven't pinned the facts to anyone yet. I'll tell them about all the things you stole, you terrible girl, and happily watch as they bring down the full force of the law upon you."

For a moment, Eleanor didn't know what to do. Her father was threatening to expose her thefts, thefts he had forced her to commit all these years. Her good name in town would be ruined, and no one would employ her. She would have nothing, and her father would have won.

I need to leave now, she realized as he stared down at her smugly, waiting for her to react. Somehow, he had guessed her intentions and was now threatening her. What better time to begin her journey?

The problem was that her father still held on to the tin with money.

He was still watching her, so, steadying her resolve, she reached out suddenly to yank the tin from his hands. He must not have expected her to act so boldly, because he only stared at her with shock as she pulled herself from his grasp and ran from the room, the tin clutched tightly from his chest.

"Eleanor!" she heard him scream from behind her as her feet slapped against the dirt. She didn't chance a look back as he continued to shout, racing as far away from him as she could get.

Chapter Three

Henry heaved a deep sigh, patting the cow firmly on her back. "Come on, Millie, I don't have all day," he told her, shaking his head at her bleating as he ushered her into the barn. It was cold out, the wind harsh and biting. She would not live through the morning if he left her out all night in the snow.

Not only would that mean he would have to find a new source of milk, but his daughter, Grace, would be devastated by the loss of the cow. Grace loved all of their farm animals, of which they had few, but the cow held a special place in her heart.

Millie continued to bleat once she was in her pen, though she did appear calmer. He gave her another small pat before heading back to the house, rubbing his freezing hands together.

Inside the cozy farmhouse, Grace was peering out the window with concern etched on her young face. She was only six years old when her mother passed away, leaving her in the care of her loving father. They had grown close over the last year, and Henry did his best to be both mother and father to the little girl. It was difficult for him. It took him longer than he liked to admit to learn how to cook and care for Grace, and there were many times when he wondered how Sarah, his late wife, had handled everything.

Grace rushed towards him as he stomped the snow off his boots, her eyes wide and filled with relief. "Is Millie alright,

Papa?" she asked, clinging to his coat and staring up at him.

"She's safe and sound in the barn, sweetheart," Henry reassured her, kneeling to be at her level. "Don't worry. I'll make sure all our animals are well cared for."

Grace smiled, her father's words providing comfort to her tender heart. Henry wrapped his arms around her, embracing her with a warm, fatherly love.

"You're the best papa in the world," Grace whispered, her voice barely audible. Her words brought joy to his heart, and he held her a little closer.

As great of a father as Grace believed him to be, she was missing a mother in her life. There was only so much Henry could teach her; in a few years, she would begin to mature, and that was when she would truly need a motherly touch. Even now, Henry worried about Grace growing up too boyish and struggling to find a husband in the future.

That, paired with him struggling alone on the farm, was what gave him the idea to look for a wife. Though he still longed for Sarah and his heart had not yet healed, both he and Grace needed a tender, loving woman in their lives. He had kept to himself in his grief, so he was unfamiliar with many of the single women in his area. He tried courting and finding a woman nearby, but they were either uninterested or had their eyes on other eligible men.

Almost desperate, he turned to the matrimonial ads and was surprised by the number of women who were just as desperate as he. He considered responding to several ads but decided against it. The way the ads were written, the women seemed desirable, and it was likely they had already received responses for their ads. Henry was not a man who would fight over a woman, so he instead chose to place an advertisement of his own and select a bride from the responses.

Unfortunately, he received no response for three months, which made him wonder if it would again just be him and Grace during the winter months. Then, there was Eleanor Monfrey.

From her letter, she seemed a solid woman. She was experienced with household chores, which interested Henry greatly. He wished she would have included more of herself in the letter so that he could better understand her personality and whether they would match, but in the end, it mattered very little. He decided to invite Eleanor to join him and his daughter.

A few weeks ago, he received a response and now was impatiently waiting. He hadn't yet informed Grace of her new mother figure in case they were not a match, but he was eager to tell her.

***

Henry sat at the kitchen table, watching Eleanor move gracefully around the room as she tidied up after dinner. He admired how she seemed to effortlessly settle into the farmhouse routine, taking care of the household tasks with a quiet determination.

She hadn't spoken much to him in the few days since her arrival other than pleasantries. She seemed to be cautious, which he understood completely. The two of them were complete strangers, and she had traveled many miles to marry him. So far, he had only tasked her with duties in the house, but she was so skilled at them that he was already considering giving her farm and garden duties as well to lighten his load.

He was pleased by the kind of woman she was, and he wasn't the only happy one. When Grace learned Eleanor was to be her new motherly figure, she was happier than he had seen her in a long time. She couldn't stop following the woman around, her eyes wide with awe as she gazed at her.

So far, this had been an excellent decision on his part.

"I want to thank you, Eleanor," Henry finally spoke, breaking the comfortable silence between them.

Eleanor turned to him, her eyes meeting his with curiosity. "For what, Henry?" she asked, her head tilting to the side somewhat.

"For being here," he said sincerely. "You've brought a light into this house that I never thought I'd see again." It was a light that had been extinguished when Sarah passed.

Eleanor smiled softly, touched by his words. "I'm grateful to be here, Henry. I'm thankful for the chance to start anew."

He nodded, his gaze returning to the floor as he tried to put his feelings into words.

"I want you to know that I'll do my best to make you feel comfortable here. It's not easy coming into a new place with strangers."

"I appreciate that," Eleanor replied, seemingly giving him her full attention. "It means a lot to me."

She was a kind woman, but there was something in her eyes that made him pause for the first time. There was an almost apprehensive look, and he had the feeling she was hiding something. He didn't believe she was a danger to his daughter, but he still felt the need to be careful.

"You know, Grace lost her mother when she was very young," Henry continued, speaking slowly and choosing his words carefully. "It's just been the two of us for a while now."

Eleanor looked up, her eyes softening with empathy. "I can't imagine how difficult that must have been for both of you," she said softly, the look of apprehension fading.

Henry nodded. "It has been, but we've managed. Grace is a wonderful child, full of joy and innocence."

Eleanor smiled warmly. "I can see that. She's a precious little girl."

"I want you to know that Grace is the most important person in my life," Henry continued. "I won't let anyone come between us or hurt her in any way."

Eleanor nodded, her sincerity evident. "I would never do anything to hurt her. I promise."

Henry appreciated her honesty, and over the next few days, he observed how

Eleanor interacted with Grace. She was patient, kind, and genuinely interested in getting to know the little girl. Grace, in turn, seemed to take a liking to Eleanor, finding a new friend in her.

So far, everything seemed to be working out.

Chapter Four

Life on Henry's farm was a new experience for Eleanor. The vast expanse of land and the simple routines of farm life were a world away from the bustling streets of the city she had left behind, though there were some similarities. There was a sense of tranquility in the countryside that she found comforting.

As the days turned into weeks, Eleanor gradually settled into her new role as a partner in Henry's life. She found joy in tending to the animals, working in the barn, and helping with the chores around the farm. She learned to appreciate the simplicity of life on the farm and the connection to nature it provided. It was much more calming than the bustling life in the city, and she immensely enjoyed all the fresh air.

What she enjoyed the most was her freedom from her father.

There was no way he would be able to track her all the way here; she had traveled a long way to get away from him. When she left home, she had hopped onto a stagecoach wagon almost immediately to get away. It felt good not having to resort to crime to get by and having her father intimidate her. She was free to be her own woman.

Readying herself, Eleanor stepped out of her bedroom and was immediately greeted by Grace, eagerly waiting outside her door. Eleanor wasn't sure how long the young girl had been there. "Good morning," Grace chirped, and Eleanor couldn't help but smile at her.

"Good morning," she murmured, reaching down to tussle her hair. "Come, let's have some oats."

Grace was the best part of Eleanor's journey across the country. Before moving, she had little to no experience with children; she never had to care for them and had never worked any jobs concerning children, though she was fond of them. Initially, she wasn't sure how to interact with the young girl, but now it was like second nature. Grace just wanted someone to talk to and play with, and Eleanor was more than happy to provide.

As the sun began to rise, Eleanor and Grace ate a filling breakfast and ventured out to the woodshed to gather firewood for the day. Henry was already awake and working in the barn, so Eleanor reserved some oats and berries for him. Grace's eyes were wide with excitement as Eleanor opened the shed, eager to spend time with Eleanor and help with the chores.

"Okay, Grace, let's see how much wood we can carry," Eleanor said, smiling down at the young girl.

Grace eagerly picked up a small log and struggled to lift it. Eleanor chuckled and bent down to help her. "Here, let me give you a hand."

Together, they began to carry armfuls of wood into the house. Grace's face lit up with delight as the two of them performed the task, chatting, and Eleanor figured the young girl realized how much fun chores could be when done with a friend.

"I like having you here, Eleanor," Grace said, her voice filled with sincerity as they tossed down the last of the wood. Eleanor clapped her hands together to dust them off. "It's more fun with you around."

Eleanor's heart warmed at Grace's words. "I like being here with you too, Grace. You make everything more special."

They continued their tasks, sharing stories and laughter along the way. Eleanor marveled at Grace's innocence and the resilience she had shown in the face of losing her mother. Their bond grew stronger with each passing minute, and Eleanor found herself cherishing the moments they spent together.

Bonding with Grace was proving to be easy, and Eleanor hoped to make some progress with Henry. The man seemed nice enough, but he kept to himself. By now, Eleanor had been present in the home for a few weeks, and he hadn't made much effort to get to know her better. Then again, she hadn't made much effort either.

Rubbing her hands together, Eleanor sat Grace in front of the fireplace to warm up while she headed back into the kitchen. As she stepped back up to the stove to warm up the oats, footsteps sounded behind her, and she turned around to see a tired-looking Henry.

He blinked at her. "Good morning," he muttered.

She froze for a moment, unsure of how to react, before springing into action. "I – yes, good morning!" She gestured for him to sit at the table and rushed to scoop some of the oats into a bowl. "It is quite cold out, is it not? I thought some oats would warm the old bones," she babbled, setting the bowl in front of him and taking the seat across from him.

A small smile crept up his lips as he scooped a bite into his mouth. "Sarah used to make oats all the time," he murmured. "They're delicious."

She stared at him as he ate, glad he genuinely enjoyed it. She longed to say more, to fill the silence, but she was unsure what to say.

He was finished before she could figure out what to say, quietly thanking her and standing. "I need to do some work in the barn," he told her, walking out of the kitchen and to the front door, where he slipped on his boots.

Eleanor followed him, still scrambling for words. "Okay! Henry, um…" He turned to look at her, his eyebrows raised, and she faltered. "I-nothing."

He has no interest in me, she thought with disappointment, feeling her shoulders sag. *Am I here just to be a mother to Grace?* It wasn't something she minded, but she also wanted a relationship with Henry.

Henry paused, and momentarily, it looked as though he wanted to say something. Eleanor grew hopeful, but then he merely nodded and headed out, closing the door behind him.

***

That evening, Eleanor found herself sitting with Henry by the fireplace. They had finished dinner some time ago, and Eleanor cleaned up while Henry got Grace ready for bed. Now, she sat on a chair performing some needlework while Henry relaxed and read a book.

Eleanor could have retired to bed long ago, but she wanted to spend some time with her husband. He may not be particularly interested in her, but she was determined to spend time with him nonetheless.

"I'm glad you're here, Eleanor," Henry said suddenly, breaking the silence.

Glancing up with surprise, she noticed his eyes were on her. His words seemed genuine, and she slowly set down her needles. *Is this it?* she wondered. *Is Henry going to show some interest in me?* "I'm glad to be here," Eleanor replied.

"I know I can be cold, and I'm sorry." He heaved a deep sigh and rubbed his face. "I'm trying to get used to having you here, but it's difficult. It hasn't been the same since Sarah's passing."

Now that she thought of it, that made sense. Of course, Henry would be distant. He was still grieving. She wasn't sure how to respond to him, so she remained silent. They sat in comfortable silence for a moment before Henry spoke again. "Sometimes, I still can't believe she's gone," he said softly, his voice tinged with sorrow.

Eleanor looked up at him, seeing the pain in his eyes. "I know, Henry," she said gently. "Losing someone you love is never easy."

Henry nodded. "Sarah was everything to me. We built this farm together and were planning a future for our family."

"I can't imagine how difficult it must have been for you," Eleanor said.

Henry sighed, his gaze fixed on the crackling flames. "I try to be strong for Grace, but there are days when the memories flood back, and it feels like I'm drowning in grief."

The pain in his eyes deepened, and Eleanor realized how deep his grief ran. It wasn't something he was going to get over anytime soon. "You don't have to be strong all the time, Henry. It's okay to feel sadness and to miss her."

He nodded, swiping at his eyes and smiling. "I know, but it's not fair to you. I'm going to try to do better for you, I promise."

Chapter Five

Eleanor's feelings for Henry and Grace deepened. She cherished the moments they spent together, their laughter, and the sense of belonging she had found on the farm. But beneath the surface of contentment, there was a persistent unease.

Henry's distant demeanor sometimes left Eleanor feeling uncertain and vulnerable. He had moments of withdrawal, retreating into the memories of his late wife, Sarah. Eleanor understood his grief, but she couldn't help but feel a pang of jealousy, knowing that she could never fully replace the woman who had been so important to him.

Still, he seemed to be more accepting of her, which made her happy. Small steps, that was what was important. He was making an effort.

Now Eleanor had encountered a new problem; Henry was showing a slight interest in her past, the life she'd lived before she joined his family. So far, she had lied and told him she had no family and had been struggling alone. He seemed to believe her; at least, she hoped he did.

Eleanor had no intention of telling him about her real past and what she'd had to resort to. She was a criminal, and she had a feeling he wouldn't take too kindly to that knowledge. She didn't want anything to jeopardize her marriage.

Currently, she was helping him with the animals in the barn. He was good with them; Eleanor had some experience handling farm animals, but not much, so he tended to the grooming and cleaning while she fed them and did other odd jobs. Due to the snow, it was getting more challenging to get to and from the barn from the farmhouse. There was more of it here than in the city; it could be as deep as her shin.

Henry and Eleanor made their way back to the farmhouse from the barn when they finished, their footsteps leaving deep imprints in the thick snow. Eleanor's boots sank with every step, making the trek more challenging. She stumbled slightly, trying to keep her balance, and Henry couldn't help but chuckle at her as he tossed a glance back.

"Careful there," he teased, flashing a mischievous grin.

Eleanor rolled her eyes playfully, feeling a mix of frustration and amusement. "Oh, hush," she retorted, attempting to regain her footing.

Seeing the opportunity for mischief, Henry scooped up a handful of snow and playfully threw it at her. It landed on her shoulder, and Eleanor gasped, feigning offense.

"Oh, you're going to pay for that," she said with a grin, quickly gathering a handful of snow to retaliate.

The snowball fight was on. Eleanor and Henry engaged in a playful exchange of snowballs, their laughter filling the crisp winter air. As they dodged and weaved through the snow, Eleanor felt the cares of the day melt away, replaced by the pure joy of the moment.

Their laughter echoed through the farmstead, and Eleanor felt a deep sense of happiness. Henry was relaxed and having a wonderful time, and so was she.

In the midst of their playful snowball fight, Eleanor caught a glimpse of movement out of the corner of her eye. She turned her head to see Henry's daughter, Grace, standing at the window of the farmhouse, watching them with delight in her eyes.

Henry noticed Eleanor's gaze and followed it to where Grace stood. He paused for a moment, his expression softening as he saw the joy on his daughter's face.

"Eleanor, look," he said, nodding towards Grace.

Eleanor turned her attention back to Grace, who was now waving at them enthusiastically. Eleanor waved back, her heart swelling with affection for the young girl. "Come join us, Grace!" Eleanor called out, inviting her to be a part of their playful snowball fight.

Grace shook her head with a grin, clearly content to watch the two of them from the warmth of the house. "We'll save some snow for you!" Henry shouted, his voice filled with mirth.

As they continued their snowball fight, Eleanor felt a sense of gratitude for the family she had found. The love and joy shared between them were unlike anything she had ever known, and she cherished every moment of it.

Eventually, the laughter subsided, and they made their way back to the farmhouse, their cheeks rosy from the cold and their spirits lifted by the playful exchange. Grace met them at the door with a warm hug for both of them.

"That was so much fun to watch!" she exclaimed, her eyes shining with happiness.

"It was, wasn't it?" Eleanor replied, smiling at Henry. "Your father sure knows how to make things fun."

Henry grinned, wrapping his arms around both Eleanor and Grace. "And I have the best company for it," he said, planting a kiss on Eleanor's forehead.

It was the first gesture of affection he had shown her, and she felt the blood rush to her cheeks in a fiery blush. What a wonderful man he was.

As they entered the warmth of the farmhouse, Eleanor felt a sense of belonging she had never known before. She had found a loving partner and a precious daughter who filled her heart with joy.

She smiled widely at Henry, her smile faltering when she noticed the deep well of sadness return. No matter how much he enjoyed himself, his grief always seemed to return.

***

That night, when the farmhouse was still and the night air whispered through the fields, Eleanor found herself grappling with her own fears. The shadows of her past loomed over her, and she couldn't shake the feeling that one day, it would come back to haunt her. She worried that her father might return, that her secrets might be revealed, and that it would shatter the life she had built with Henry and Grace.

She knew she had changed and grown since those dark days, but the fear of judgment and rejection lingered in the back of her mind. She worried that someone from her past might come looking for her, threatening the life she had worked so hard to build.

Lost in her thoughts, Eleanor wished she had a father like Henry – a man who loved and accepted her unconditionally, a man who had shown her what it meant to be cared for and cherished. The contrast between her father's past manipulation and Henry's kindness was stark, and she longed for the kind of love that Henry showered upon Grace.

Eleanor was sitting by the window, lost in her thoughts. Grace was asleep, and Henry was out in the barn, checking on the animals one last time. She looked up as he reentered the house, shrugging out of his coat and shivering. Their eyes met, and his gaze softened.

"Eleanor," he murmured, walking over to her and taking the seat next to her. "Why do I get the sense something is wrong?"

Because there is. Eleanor took a deep breath, unsure of how to put her feelings into words. "I... I have grown to love you and

Grace so much, Henry. But there are times when I feel like I'm just an outsider, like there's a part of you that I can't reach."

Henry sighed, his eyes reflecting a mixture of emotions. "I'm trying, Eleanor, I truly am. This is still difficult for me, you know." He reached out and settled his hand atop hers, squeezing. The gesture warmed her heart, even with the chill emanating from him. "I care for you, too. I just need a bit more time."

She nodded with understanding, feeling a bit better. Knowing that Henry did, in fact, care about her was wonderful to hear, and it gave her the strength to keep going. "I can be patient."

Chapter Six

As time continued to pass, Eleanor's presence became a vital part of Henry and Grace's lives. She effortlessly slipped into the role of a caring mother figure, and Grace's face would light up with joy whenever Eleanor entered the room. They would spend hours playing together, reading books, and simply enjoying each other's company.

Eleanor brought new life and laughter to their home. Grace was blossoming under her care, becoming more confident and curious about the world around her. The bond between Grace and Eleanor grew stronger with each passing day, and it warmed Henry's heart to see them together.

Truly, Eleanor had been a good choice.

She was a wonderful woman, and he immensely enjoyed her company. Sometimes, thoughts of his wife intruded, and he retreated; other times, Eleanor's sweet smile and laugh were enough to distract him. He knew he would move on one day, and thoughts of Sarah would no longer bring him pain, but he wasn't ready to give up her memory yet.

Eleanor had promised she would be patient, and Henry told himself he wouldn't make her wait long.

Henry hitched the horses to the wagon, preparing for the trip into town. Winter had long since settled in, and he wanted to make sure they had enough supplies to last through the harsh weather that could be unpredictable in these parts. Eleanor and Grace were joining him on the trip, their excitement palpable. It was Eleanor's first trip into town.

Grace chatted animatedly as they rode into town, eager to explore the stores and see the decorations. Henry smiled at her enthusiasm and promised her a piece of candy if she behaved herself.

They stepped down from the wagon at the general store, and Henry led the way inside. He gathered the essential supplies, carefully considering what they might need in case of a snowstorm. In the past, there were times when he and Grace were trapped inside due to heavy snow, and he wanted to be prepared in case it occurred again.

He noticed Eleanor's thoughtful expressions as she looked at various items, trailing her fingers along tins and bins.

As he turned to grab some canned goods, he noticed Eleanor almost subconsciously slipping a bag of sweets into her petticoat. His heart sank, and he felt a wave of disappointment wash over him. He was intensely against criminal behavior and wondered how he hadn't noticed this type of behavior from her before.

Without making a scene, Henry quietly approached her and whispered, "Put it back, Eleanor. We don't need that."

Her face flushed with embarrassment, Eleanor quickly complied, placing the bag back on the shelf. She avoided his gaze, knowing she had been caught, her cheeks a deep pink. Grace, oblivious to it all, begged for one of the wooden dolls.

Once they were back in the wagon and heading home, Henry couldn't ignore the issue any longer. He took a deep breath and spoke gently but firmly, "Eleanor, I saw what you did back there."

Her eyes filled with shame, and she looked down at her hands. "I'm sorry, Henry. It's just... It's something I used to do from time to time in order to survive."

This was new information to him. "You had to do terrible things like that?" What kind of life had she led? he wondered as she nodded. Was she always hungry and homeless, and that was why she had to resort to such behavior? *I probably would have learned this sooner if I had pried a bit more into her past.*

He decided he would not hold this against her. She made a mistake, simple as that. "I understand it's not easy to break old habits," he said softly. "But stealing is not the way anymore. We have each other, and we'll make sure you never have to resort to that again."

Eleanor nodded, her voice barely above a whisper. "I'm so sorry for disappointing you."

Henry squeezed her hand reassuringly. "You haven't disappointed me, Eleanor. I just want you to be open with me, to trust me with your struggles. We'll face them together."

She nodded, tears spilling down her cheeks. "Thank you for understanding, Henry. I promise I'll do my best to change."

***

The farmhouse became a bustling hub of festive preparations as Christmas drew near. Eleanor and Grace spent their days baking cookies in the warm kitchen, filling the air with the sweet scent of vanilla and cinnamon. They laughed and sang to one another while rolling out the dough and cutting it into various shapes.

Henry couldn't help but smile as he watched the two of them work together. Their laughter was infectious, and he found himself joining in, feeling the weight of his worries and reservations lifting in the presence of their joy.

Together, they adorned the house with garlands made of greens and bright red berries, turning the simple farmhouse into a cozy winter wonderland. Grace's eyes shone excitedly as they decorated a Christmas tree, stringing berries and hanging handmade wooden ornaments made over the last few days.

Evening came, and they gathered around the fireplace, sipping warm tea and admiring the tree. They exchanged stories, sharing memories of Christmases past, and creating new ones together. It was a perfect evening, filled with love and laughter, and Henry found himself caught up in the joy of the moment.

He was drawn to Eleanor's beauty and infectious laughter in the candlelight. Perhaps it was the spirit of the season or his growing feelings, but he was quite fond of her.

But as the night wore on, a twinge of guilt began to creep into his heart. He hadn't thought about his late wife, Sarah, as much as he usually did during the holiday season. It had become a tradition for him to reminisce about their past Christmases together, but this year, Eleanor and Grace had brought such happiness into his life that he had let his guard down and forgotten to honor Sarah's memory.

Feeling uncomfortable, Henry excused himself and wished Eleanor and Grace a good night. He retired to his bedroom, where the soft glow of a single candle illuminated a small portrait of Sarah. Gazing at her face, he felt a mixture of gratitude for the new love he had found and sorrow for the love he had lost.

He whispered to the portrait, "I'm sorry, Sarah. I didn't mean to forget you tonight. Eleanor and Grace have become such an important part of my life, and I let myself get carried away in the joy of the moment."

Tears welled up in his eyes as he remembered the life they had shared, the memories they had made. He missed her dearly but also knew that life had to move on. He couldn't deny the love he had found with Eleanor and the happiness she brought to their home.

Taking a deep breath, Henry resolved to honor Sarah's memory while cherishing the new chapter of his life with Eleanor and Grace. He knew he could love them both in different ways and that it didn't diminish the love he felt for his late wife.

As he lay in bed, he found comfort in the knowledge that love had a way of expanding the heart, making room for new connections without erasing the old ones. He vowed to share stories of Sarah with Eleanor and Grace so they, too, could feel a part of the woman who had shaped him into the man he was today.

With a renewed sense of peace, Henry closed his eyes, grateful for the love surrounding him and the memories that would forever hold a place in his heart. And on this night, he knew he had been blessed with a gift beyond measure: a family that brought warmth, love, and joy into his life.

Chapter Seven

Eleanor was in the midst of making a stew when Henry entered the kitchen. "Eleanor? Do you have a moment?" he asked.

She turned towards him immediately, abandoning the stew. "Absolutely!" she gushed with a grin, ready to give him her full attention. Over the last few days, he had been improving in his behavior towards her and was making more of an effort to speak with her. This not only made her happy, but it gave her hope that they would have a good marriage.

"An errand boy just stopped by with a message. There's an older man in town asking around for you. Do you know who it might be?"

It was as if the world around her was collapsing. She was frozen in place, her smile now forced. "An older man?" she repeated.

He nodded. "Someone you know?"

She shrugged, doing her best to remain calm while she screamed inwardly. "Did the man give a name?" Her father's name was Charles.

He shook his head. "Not that I know of. I'm going into town to run some last-minute errands. Would you like to accompany me?"

Eleanor wanted to tell him no because she feared this older man was indeed her father. Henry knew she had stolen from time to time, but he didn't know her full past, nor did she want him to. "Sure."

Her heart sank as she recognized the man who had brought misery to her life for so many years messily eating at one of the restaurants. True to his word, Henry was off running errands, leaving her to speak with her father.

He looked the same as when she left him, except the bruises had long faded. She gave him a dirty look as she settled in the seat across from him. Eleanor had left her past behind when she ventured West, hoping to start anew and escape the painful memories of her difficult childhood. Her father had been a dishonest man, forcing his daughter into a life of thievery to survive.

"I found you, Ellie," Charles sneered, using the nickname he had given her when she was a child. "I knew you'd make something of yourself, marrying into money and living the good life here."

Eleanor tried to compose herself, not wanting to reveal the anxiety bubbling inside her. She took a deep breath to steady her nerves. "I've left that life behind, Father," she said firmly, trying to maintain her composure. "I'm a different person now, and I won't go back to the way things were."

Charles laughed, a bitter sound that sent shivers down Eleanor's spine. "You can't escape your past, Ellie. I know what you used to do, and I'm sure the good folks of this town would be interested to hear about it."

Eleanor's heart raced, fearing the shame and judgment that could come from her past being exposed. She had worked hard to build a respectable life with Henry and Grace, and she didn't want her past to taint the happiness they had found together.

"What do you want, Father?" she asked, her voice trembling slightly. She couldn't let him destroy the life she had built with Henry and Grace. She knew she had to find a way to get him out of their lives for good.

"I want what's rightfully mine," Charles replied coldly. "You owe me for all those years you spent stealing for me. I want a cut of what you've got now."

"Don't be ridiculous," Eleanor replied, mustering all the strength she had. "I'm here because I wanted a fresh start, away from all the things you made me do, not because Henry has money."

"What about me?" her father snapped, not even attempting to keep his voice down. "You up and left me with nothing. You were a real moneymaker for me back then, and now I'm surviving on scraps while you enjoy your life. That doesn't seem very fair to me."

Eleanor felt sick to her stomach. She had worked so hard to leave that life behind, and now he was threatening to drag her back into it. She didn't have much money, but she was willing to do whatever it took to protect her newfound family.

"I'll get you some money, but you have to promise to leave and never come back," she said firmly.

Charles chuckled darkly. "Oh, I'll take your money, but I can't promise I won't come back. A woman like you can always find a way to make more."

Eleanor felt a sense of hopelessness wash over her. She knew that dealing with her father would be an ongoing battle, and she feared the repercussions if he revealed her past to Henry and the townspeople.

As she returned to the farmhouse later that day with her husband, her mind was heavy with worry. She couldn't bear the thought of losing the life she had built with Henry and Grace. She had to find a way to protect them, even if it meant confronting her painful past. But for now, she kept her secrets hidden, hoping to find a solution before her father could carry out his threats.

Chapter Eight

The snowstorm had arrived with a vengeance, blanketing the farm in a deep and cold embrace. Eleanor stood by the window, watching as the snowflakes fell gracefully from the sky. It was a winter wonderland, but she knew that the beauty outside came with its own set of challenges.

As the morning light peeked through the curtains, Henry and Eleanor bundled up in warm clothes and stepped outside to tend to the animals. The snow was knee-deep, making their movements slow and deliberate. The animals were huddled together for warmth, and Eleanor felt a pang of concern for their well-being.

"We'll have to make sure they have enough food and water," Henry said, his breath forming a cloud of steam in the cold air.

Eleanor nodded, her cheeks flushed from the chill. "I'll help you bring some hay and water to the barn," she replied, determined to do her part.

Together, they trudged through the snow, carrying bales of hay and buckets of water for the animals. It was hard work, but Eleanor was grateful that there was little to no damage to the farm. The barn had held up well against the storm, and the animals seemed to be in good spirits despite the cold.

As the day wore on, the snow continued to fall relentlessly. Eleanor and Henry took turns keeping the fire in the farmhouse stoked, trying to keep the cold at bay. Grace spent her time inside, playing with her toys and looking out the window with wonder at the white landscape.

"It's beautiful, isn't it?" Henry said, sitting by the fireplace with Eleanor.

She nodded, her eyes fixed on the dancing flames. "It is, but it's also a reminder of how unpredictable nature can be."

Henry placed his hand on hers, offering comfort. "We'll get through this."

She couldn't help but worry about their neighbors and the townsfolk.

"Everything alright, Eleanor?"

"Yes, I was just thinking about the neighbors and how they're faring in this storm," she replied, pulling her shawl tighter around her shoulders.

He nodded, understanding her concern. "I'm sure they're doing their best to weather the storm, just like we are," he reassured her. "We'll help them if they need it, just as they would help us."

As the evening approached, the snowfall showed no signs of letting up. Eleanor knew they would need to continue tending to the animals and keeping the farmhouse warm. The cold and isolation outside made her appreciate the warmth and togetherness inside even more.

***

The snowstorm let up a few days later, and the two of them finally got word from town.

The inn, where many travelers sought refuge, couldn't withstand the weight of the snow on its roof, and it collapsed under the pressure. The guests, including her father, were left with nowhere to go but the church. The community rallied together, providing shelter and warmth for those stranded in the storm.

The snowstorm had been relentless, leaving the town and surrounding areas covered in a thick blanket of snow. The roads were blocked, and supplies couldn't get through. As the news spread, the townsfolk came together to help those stranded and in need.

Eleanor, Henry, and Grace were among those who ventured out in the bitter cold to offer their assistance. They loaded the wagon with whatever wood and food they could spare from the farm and set off towards the church. As they arrived, they saw that others had already gathered, bringing their own contributions to aid the guests who had sought refuge there.

Eleanor felt a mixture of emotions when she noticed her father among the people seeking shelter. She tried to avoid him, not wanting to engage in conversation or risk his recent threats resurfacing. But as she worked alongside the townsfolk, her father's presence weighed on her mind. *Is he going to blackmail me in front of everyone?* she worried. *Am I going to have to start my life over somewhere else?*

Despite her worries, she noticed that her father kept to himself, seemingly engrossed in his own thoughts. The kindness and compassion surrounding him seemed to leave an impression, and Eleanor felt both relieved and concerned.

Henry watched Eleanor with admiration as she tirelessly helped those in need. He didn't know the man she was avoiding was her father, but he could see the concern in her eyes. She did her best to hide it, but knew she didn't do a very good job.

I hope everything turns out alright.

Chapter Nine

Two days before Christmas, Eleanor knew she could no longer keep her secrets hidden.

By then, the townsfolk were able to take care of themselves, so Eleanor, Grace, and Henry no longer needed to go into town and help them. This meant she had not seen her father in a few days and did not know what he was planning.

The weight of her past deeds weighed heavily on her heart, and she knew it was time to come clean to Henry. There was the chance he would disapprove and never forgive her. While the thought was a terrifying one, she needed to be honest with her husband.

She found him sitting by the fireplace, gazing into the crackling flames, lost in thought. Taking a deep breath, Eleanor mustered her courage and sat down beside him. "Henry, there's something I need to tell you," she began, her voice trembling with emotion.

Henry turned to her, his eyes filled with concern. "What is it, Eleanor? You can tell me anything."

With tears welling up in her eyes, Eleanor confessed everything. She told him about her past life with her father, how he had taught her to steal and forced her into a life of crime. She spoke of the guilt and shame she had carried with her for so long, of the fear that her past would ruin the life she had built with him and Grace.

Henry listened attentively as she poured her heart out, his expression unwavering. When she finally finished, she waited anxiously for his response, fearing that her confession would change everything between them. *He's going to throw me out, I'm sure of it.* She had no clue what she would do after or where she would go, but she could rest easy knowing she had been honest with the one she loved.

But to her surprise, Henry reached out and gently took her hand in his. "Eleanor, I already know," he said, his voice steady and reassuring.

Eleanor looked at him, her eyes wide with shock. Out of all the things he could have said, she wasn't expecting that. "You know?" she repeated.

Henry nodded. "Your father came to see me a few days ago. He wanted me to know the truth and to take all the blame for your past. He came here intending to blackmail you, but he left with a different perspective."

"He... he took the blame for me?" Eleanor stammered, her heart touched by the unexpected turn of events. That wasn't like her father at all. What had changed him? Or was this another part of his plan?

"Yes," Henry replied with a soft smile. "He realized that what you did in the past did not reflect who you are now. He saw the person you've become, the woman who worked hard to escape her past and build a new life for herself and for us. He wanted me to know that you earned your own money to travel out West, that you've changed and grown."

Eleanor was overwhelmed with a mix of emotions—relief, gratitude, and even a hint of forgiveness towards her father. She never thought he would take responsibility for her actions or understand the changes she had gone through.

"He said he wanted to celebrate the person you've become, not destroy it," Henry continued. "He still cares for you, Eleanor, in his own way."

Eleanor wiped away tears of gratitude, feeling a weight lift off her shoulders. "I never thought he could be capable of such understanding," she admitted.

Henry wrapped his arms around her, pulling her close. "People can surprise us,

Eleanor. What matters now is that we're together, and we're here for each other."

In the warmth of Henry's embrace, Eleanor felt a newfound sense of peace. The truth was out, and he still loved and accepted her. Their love had weathered the storm of her past, and now, they could face the future together.

Chapter Ten

In the days following their heartfelt conversation, Eleanor and Henry found a renewed sense of freedom and joy. Eleanor was relieved to have her past laid bare and be accepted by the man she loved. Henry, too, had come to understand that holding on to guilt and regret would only hold him back from fully embracing the happiness that lay before him.

The days leading up to Christmas were filled with preparations and excitement. Grace's eyes sparkled with wonder as they decorated the tree, hung stockings by the fireplace, and prepared a feast fit for a joyful celebration.

On Christmas day, the farmhouse was filled with warmth and laughter. Eleanor felt a sense of joy and contentment in the home she had come to love.

She hummed to herself as she set the table where Henry and Grace were gathered, eagerly awaiting Christmas dinner. She had worked hard on it for the last day and was proud of how everything had turned out.

As she set the last plate down, a knock sounded from the front door. She shot a curious glance at Henry, who was whispering to Grace, and moved to answer it. Eleanor's heart skipped a beat when she saw a figure standing at the doorstep. It was her father, Charles, the man from her past whom she had feared and tried to escape.

Her initial instinct was to be wary, but as she looked at him, she saw a different man than the one she remembered. His shoulders were slumped, and there was a vulnerability in his eyes that she hadn't seen before. He appeared quieter and gentler, as if life had worn away the harshness he once held. Who was this man standing before her?

"Eleanor," he said softly, his voice tinged with regret. "I hope you can find it in your heart to forgive me."

Eleanor's heart was conflicted, torn between the memories of the past and the sight of a changed man standing before her. She hesitated for a moment before finally finding her voice. "Come in," she said, motioning for him to join them at the table.

Grace looked up with curiosity, not fully understanding the complexity of the situation but sensing the tension in the air. Henry, too, noticed the unease and offered a reassuring smile to Eleanor.

As they settled at the table, Eleanor's father looked around, taking in the warmth and love that permeated the farmhouse. "You have a beautiful home here," he said, his voice sincere.

"Thank you," Eleanor replied, unsure of how to fully process her father's presence.

"I know I haven't been the best father to you," he continued, his gaze fixed on Eleanor. "I've made mistakes, and I can't change the past, but I'm trying to be a better man now."

Eleanor searched his eyes for sincerity, and for the first time, she saw a glimmer of remorse that touched her heart.

Henry spoke up, breaking the tension in the room. "Well, we all have our pasts," he said, his voice gentle. "What's important is how we choose to move forward."

Eleanor's father nodded, his gaze dropping to his hands. "I just want you to have a loving and happy marriage, Eleanor. And it seems like you've found that here."

She glanced at Henry, feeling a rush of gratitude for the man who had shown her the meaning of love and acceptance.

"We've had our share of struggles, but we're working through them together," Henry replied, his hand finding Eleanor's under the table.

Eleanor's father nodded again, seemingly lost in his thoughts. "I'm sorry for the trouble I caused you, Eleanor," he said, his voice barely above a whisper.

Eleanor took a deep breath, trying to find the strength to let go of the past. "I accept your apology, father," she said, using the term she had rarely used before. "But let's focus on the present and the future."

He looked up at her, and a hint of a smile appeared on his lips. "Thank you, Eleanor."

As they enjoyed their Christmas dinner, Eleanor found herself experiencing a mix of emotions. She was still wary of her father's presence, but she also felt a glimmer of hope that perhaps he had truly changed.

As the evening unfolded, Eleanor realized that this Christmas was about forgiveness and second chances. And she felt grateful for the new beginnings unfolding in the presence of her loving husband, her daughter, and even her father.

Throughout the meal, Grace chattered happily about her Christmas presents and the snowman she had built outside. Eleanor smiled as she watched her daughter and father interact, amazed at the bond forming between them.

During dessert, Eleanor's father cleared his throat, drawing the attention of everyone at the table. "I want to say something," he said, his eyes meeting Eleanor's.

She nodded, encouraging him to speak.

"I've spent most of my life doing wrong, making mistakes that have hurt others," he began. "But I'm grateful for this chance to see the life you've built, Eleanor. You've grown into a remarkable woman, and I couldn't be prouder."

Tears welled up in Eleanor's eyes, and she reached for her father's hand. "Thank you, father. I never thought we would reach this point, but I'm so glad you're here with us."

Henry also offered a nod of acceptance, understanding that this was an important moment for Eleanor. "Thank you for joining us, Charles," he said sincerely. "We all have our pasts, but what matters now is the future we choose to build."

After their meal, as the warmth of the fireplace enveloped them, Henry looked at Eleanor's father with a genuine expression of concern. "You're welcome to stay with us, you know," he offered. "We have plenty of room, and Grace would love to have you around."

Eleanor's father hesitated, his eyes filled with gratitude, but he shook his head. "I appreciate the offer, but I don't want to impose on your family," he replied. "I have a stagecoach ticket to return home, and I should be on my way."

Henry nodded, understanding the sentiment. "If you change your mind, know that our door is always open to you," he said sincerely.

Eleanor's father nodded in appreciation, a hint of emotion in his eyes. "Thank you, Henry. You've been kinder to me than I deserve."

Henry smiled warmly. "We all make mistakes, but it's never too late to start anew. If you're serious about changing, consider finding permanent lodging in town. It's a fresh start, and you'll be closer to Eleanor and Grace."

Eleanor's father seemed touched by the suggestion.

Eleanor listened quietly, torn between the past and the possibility of a better future for her father. She had spent so much of her life running away from him and the pain he had caused, but now she felt a glimmer of hope that he could change.

As the evening wore on, Eleanor's father eventually bid them farewell, promising to think about Henry's suggestion. Henry shook his hand warmly, and Grace offered him a hesitant but sweet goodbye hug.

After her father had left, Eleanor turned to Henry, her heart full of emotions. "Thank you for being so understanding," she said softly.

Henry wrapped his arms around her, pulling her close. "We're a family, Eleanor," he replied. "And family takes care of each other, even if it's not always easy."

She nodded, feeling a sense of peace settling over her. Henry's acceptance of her father, even in the face of their complicated history, filled her with gratitude.

"I don't know what the future holds for him," Eleanor said, resting her head on Henry's shoulder. "But I hope he finds the strength to change, like you said."

"He's taken the first step by acknowledging his past mistakes," Henry said. "And I truly believe that with time and effort, people can change."

Eleanor looked up at Henry, her heart swelling with love and admiration for the man by her side. "You've given me so much, Henry," she said, her voice trembling with emotion. "Not just love and a home, but also the belief that people can change and find redemption."

Henry smiled, brushing a gentle kiss on her forehead. "We're in this together, Eleanor," he said. "And no matter what challenges come our way, we'll face them as a family."

At that moment, Eleanor knew that her past no longer defined her, and she was free to embrace the love and happiness that had found her in the West. With Henry and Grace by her side, she felt a sense of belonging she had never known before.

Eleanor knew that the true gift she had received was the gift of love, forgiveness, and a family that embraced her for who she was. And at that moment, she couldn't have asked for anything more.

The End

FREE GIFT

Just to say thanks for checking our works we like to gift you

Our Exclusive Never Before Released Books

100% FREE!

Please GO TO

`http://cleanromancepublishing.com/gift`

And get your FREE gift

Thanks for being such a wonderful client.

Please Check out My Other Works

By checking out the link below

http://cleanromancepublishing.com/fjauth

Thank You

Many thanks for taking the time to buy and read through this book.

It means lots to be supported by SPECIAL readers like YOU.

Hope you enjoyed the book; please support my writing by leaving an honest review to assist other readers.

.

With Regards,

Faith Johnson

Printed in Great Britain
by Amazon

34244171R00065